SCOOBY-DOO!

STEALS THE DOG SHOW

Written by Sonia Sander
Illustrated by Alcadia SNC

ABDOPUBLISHING.COM

Reinforced library bound edition published in 2016 by Spotlight, a division of ABDO
PO Box 398166, Minneapolis, Minnesota 55439. Spotlight produces high-quality
reinforced library bound editions for schools and libraries. Published by agreement
with Warner Bros. Entertainment Inc.

Printed in the United States of America, North Mankato, Minnesota.
092015
012016

CATALOGING-IN-PUBLICATION DATA

Sander, Sonia.
 Scooby-Doo steals the dog show / Sonia Sander.
  p. cm. (Scooby-Doo leveled readers)
 Summary: A crazy canine spook is terrorizing the dog show. Shaggy and Scooby prove which
 dog is best in show.
 1. Scooby-Doo (Fictitious character)--Juvenile fiction. 2. Dogs--Juvenile fiction. 3. Mystery and
 detective stories--Juvenile fiction. 4. Adventure and adventures--Juvenile fiction.
 [Fic]--dc23
                         2015156082

 978-1-61479-421-9   (Reinforced Library Bound Edition)

Spotlight
A Division of ABDO
abdopublishing.com

The gang was eager to see behind the scenes at the Perfect Pooch Show.

"Like, I bet Scoob could win!" said Shaggy, as the gang got their dog show tickets.

"Come on, gang," said Fred.

"The Secrets of the Dog Show tour is starting."

All the dogs were spoiled rotten.
Shaggy and Scooby snuck in for a snack.
"Like, this is the life, right Scoob?" asked Shaggy.
"Ruh-huh!" said Scooby.

Just then, a loud howl rang out.
"Jeepers," said Daphne. "What was that?"
No one had to wait long to find out.
A phantom dog ran in and stole a toy poodle.

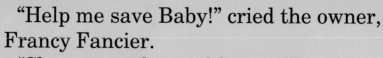

"Help me save Baby!" cried the owner,
Francy Fancier.
"She means the world to me!"
"Don't worry," said Fred.
"We'll find Baby."

"Jinkies," said Velma, looking at Baby's things.
"That phantom didn't leave one clue."
"Like, we tried our best," said Shaggy.
"I think it's time to go home."

The rest of the gang wasn't giving up so easily.
"No, Scooby needs to enter the show," said
Fred.

It took a few Scooby Snacks but Scooby agreed.

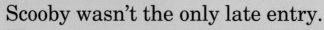

Scooby wasn't the only late entry.

"I'm sorry we are so late," said the owner of a pink toy poodle.

"Little Poppy wasn't feeling well."

Poppy didn't look like a show dog.
But no one could keep their eyes off her.
She was so pretty.

Shaggy did his best to find the right look for Scooby.

It took a while but finally Scooby was perfect.

Francy helped Fred, Daphne and Velma look for clues. They talked to the head groomer, Grady Glitter, first.

Francy never liked Grady and Grady never liked Francy. They could never agree on how to groom Baby.

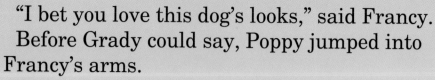

"I bet you love this dog's looks," said Francy.
Before Grady could say, Poppy jumped into Francy's arms.

Grady quickly grabbed Poppy back.

As he did, Velma spied a stripe of pink on his jacket.

"My Baby used to kiss me like that,"
cried Francy.
"Don't worry," said Daphne. "We'll find her."

Before long, the loud howl was back.
OW-OW-OW-OW-OW!
And so was the phantom dog.

This time the phantom dog was after Scooby.

"Like, I think we'd better run for it, Scoob!" cried Shaggy.

The phantom dog was hot on the gang's trail. No matter which way they turned, they couldn't lose him.

"Quick, gang!" called Fred.

"Let's hide behind Grady's curtains!"

Safe at last, Shaggy and Scooby had a bit of fun.

"Like, check out Scoob's new look," said Shaggy.

"I think I've seen that moustache before," said Velma.

"I think it's time we trapped that phantom," said Fred.

"The next time we see him, we're going to be ready."

An hour later, the phantom dog was after Scooby again.

This time the gang was ready for him! Thanks to a giant wall of hair dryers, the phantom dog had nowhere to hide.

Tired of fighting the hair dryers, Grady fell to the floor.

"The pink dye and the moustache gave you away," said Velma.

"If it weren't for you meddling kids," said Grady.

"I could have won this show and opened my dream dog salon!"

"Thank you for saving my Baby,"
said Francy.
"In our eyes, you're both Best in Show!"
Scooby-Dooby-Doo!

32